HEAT WAVES

A M/M FANTASY ROMANCE NOVELETTE

RYLEY BANKS

This is a work of fiction. Names, characters, businesses, organizations, places, events, and incidents are the products of the author's imagination or used in a fictitious manner. Any resemblance to any actual persons, living or dead, or actual events, is purely coincidental. No part of this work was generated by artificial intelligence technologies. No persons or animals, living or dead, were harmed by the writing of this book.

Copyright © 2023 by Ryley Banks

All rights reserved.

This book or any portion thereof may not be reproduced, stored in a retrieval system, transmitted in any form or by any electronic or mechanical means (including storage and retrieval systems), or used in any manner whatsoever without the express written permission of the author or publisher, except for the use of brief quotations in a book review.

No part of this book may be used in any manner for purposes of training artificial intelligence (AI) technologies to generate audio or text, including without limitation, technologies that are capable of generating works in the same style or genre as this work without the specific and express permission from the author.

Published by Three Lemon Press, LLC

ISBN: 978-1-962835-00-8 (ebook) | 978-1-962835-01-5 (paperback)

Editor: Red Quill Editing, LLC

Cover: Leslie Morris Noyes

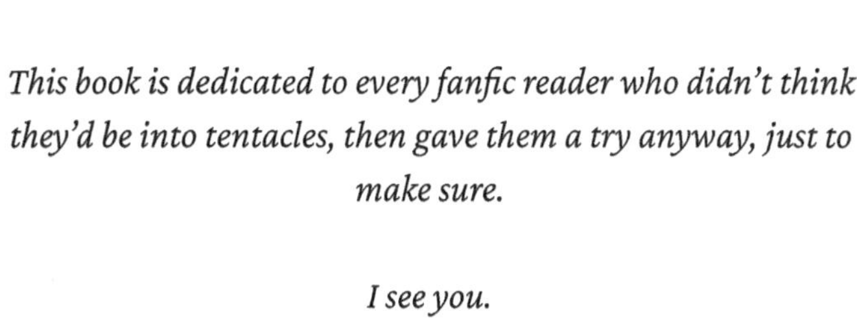

This book is dedicated to every fanfic reader who didn't think they'd be into tentacles, then gave them a try anyway, just to make sure.

I see you.

xoxo Ryley

ONE

The elf's whisper-quiet steps should have kept him well hidden. And they would—but not from me. His long brown hair was swept back and tied out of his way. My mouth watered. What if I gave in to the urge to sink my pointed canines into his neck, dragging them down the flesh to hear him cry out? My body tensed, eager to take take take. No. It wasn't time. But soon, he'd remember he belonged to me.

"Did you see that?" I froze, my long fingers stretched toward a low hanging bunch of nectar fruit. I gestured with my chin. "Over there."

Vulen, my assistant, turned his gaze toward the tree line. Nothing moved, though I was certain I'd seen an unnatural shadow. "I'm sorry, Kalysin. I must have missed it."

His gray eyes swept back to me. "Perhaps you should have a drink of water. It's been so hot and dry—"

"I'm fine"—*absolutely not hallucinating, or insane, or seeing things*—"unlike these nectar fruit. They should be smooth, shiny. A vibrant green. But this whole orchard is sickly." I touched the cluster of fruit, and half of them dropped to the ground, joining countless others. I picked up several and gave them to Vulen, who labeled and packed them away for inspection.

Lord Elmar had demanded I meet with him that morning about the crops. I'd rushed in late, meeting Vulen at the door. Lord Elmar had been in his conservatory.

"What am I giving you coin for, Kalysin, as my Overseer of Lands, if you don't actually *oversee*?" He clenched a freshly picked furry yellow fruit in his hand so hard the fruit's skin began to split, separating from the flesh. "Consequences, Kalysin, and dire ones, if this continues —your tardiness and the deteriorating harvest. You should be able to do *something* since your own lands are producing. We all must make sacrifices." He dropped the mangled fruit, and it hit the marble floor with a muffled wet thud. A servant swept in and cleaned up every trace.

I'd bowed in acquiescence, unwilling to brave Lord Elmar's reaction if I told him the reason I was late was because his messenger had notified me at an ungodly early hour, and I'd arrived as soon as I could.

As Vulen and I finished with the nectar fruit orchard, taking a few more samples, I panicked over what to tell

Lord Elmar. What were samples of crops going to show, other than the simple fact the plants weren't getting enough water?

"We're going to the brambleberries next?" Vulen asked, adjusting his water packs.

"Yes." Lord Elmar had also made it clear our rate of crop monitoring was unsatisfactory. "I don't want another meeting like this morning's if we can help it."

"I was afraid he would strike you," Vulen whispered as we made our way across Lord Elmar's vast lands to the next planted plot, our sandaled feet kicking up a plume of dust behind us as though the ground didn't remember what it was like to be wet.

"Me too," I admitted. "But it's no matter. I'm fortunate Lord Elmar gave me a position other than as a servant or messenger." Or so I kept reminding myself.

The brambleberry bushes were planted in interminably long tracts. We settled under a scrubby tree that provided some shade about halfway down one of the lines. Vulen removed the packs he carried and wiped the sweat from his forehead. I drank from my waterskin, half empty already. I swallowed, then knelt in the sandy dirt, peering under the lowest brambleberry branches. A concerning number of hard, green-white fruit. After carefully plucking two of the few ripe black ones, I offered Vulen one and popped the other in my mouth. The sweet, tangy juice rushed over my tongue, and I closed my eyes, taking brief joy in one of the few perks of my work. I hummed, transported back to my time as a youngling, raiding my mother's brambleberry bushes with— My brows knit together. I couldn't recall my playmate's features, much less their name.

But the headache I had from the effort to remember was very real indeed. They'd been happening increasingly often, as were the dreams slipping through my mind like a handful of seawater as soon as I woke each morning.

"Are you well, Kalysin?" Vulen asked, his head tilted to the side.

"No. This damned heat." I spit out a seed that had lodged in my teeth. "Let's get this over with."

We trudged onward, the top branches of the long, staked rows of thorny bushes repeating the same story as the lower ones with the addition of curled, sun-scorched leaves.

"Do you remember when it last rained?" I asked Vulen.

He frowned. "I—maybe late spring? Or perhaps it was early spring." Vulen stared off in the distance, over the rolling hills and the cloudless blue sky.

"I can't remember either," I admitted. The rains had not come this summer to fill the streams and rivers to bursting like they had in the past, yet I'd held out hope the drought hadn't affected the crops. Between the brambleberries, the nectar fruit earlier, and the sickly patches of spike melons we'd inspected before them, this was nothing like I'd ever seen.

The midday summer sun burned my tanned arms, but my skin prickled as though a winter chill had blown in. Someone was watching me.

Not us.

Me.

I scanned the landscape, pulse galloping. There, by the trees—a shadow darker than the others, deeper, like it absorbed the light.

I turned to Vulen and startled when he grabbed me first, a death grip on my arm. "Over there," he whispered, pointing with his other hand, not to the forest, but to the top of a nearby hill.

A group of robed and masked figures swayed and gestured, their arcane chanting barely reaching my keen ears. Green light flared in between each figure, shooting to the sky like lightning in reverse.

"Who are they?" Vulen still hadn't let go of my arm.

"Mages," I whispered back. Green light blazed again. "Powerful ones."

The group went silent and turned toward us in unison, as though each one was controlled by the same brain. Their heads tilted, arms outstretched, and then—

"We need to go. *Now.*" I grabbed Vulen's arm with one hand and whirled back. In my haste, I scraped my other hand against a stray brambleberry branch. The thorns tore into my skin like knives, ripping thin scratches across the back of my hand. I hissed as blood welled from the lines, immediately beginning to sting. I grabbed a piece of cloth from my pocket and wrapped my hand. The cuts would clot quickly—it was the irritating substance the thorns were coated in that would bother me more. My skin would turn red, swell, and itch for the better part of a week, all due to my own carelessness.

I cursed, and my hands shook as we sped back to the path. How did the mages know we were there? Had they somehow heard us? What were they doing? And how had they gotten onto Lord Elmar's lands undetected? Magic-wielders were rare enough on their own; a group of them was nearly unheard of.

I snuck glances toward the trees. But neither the deep shadow nor the mages were anywhere to be seen. I exhaled, my body unwinding in relief at not being followed.

"Go home," I told Vulen. "And keep your eyes open."

He nodded anxiously, eyes wide, before he took off toward the main gate.

I inhaled, forcing my muscles to relax as I hastened down the trail toward the smaller gate I frequented. Sweat trickled down my temple, and I wiped it away with my bandaged hand. Two guards at the gate nodded to me, and I gave them a short wave, barely holding it together as I swiftly left the estate and headed home along the shoreline path.

Lord Elmar's lands were on a plateau, and my way home was downhill for the most part. The air cooled as the land returned to its uncultivated state, the road winding through thickets and scrub, the trees set far enough back from the dirt path to not hinder a traveler's wagon or cart. Here, the lands appeared more lush, greener, dense.

I could *breathe* again.

The closer I was to home, the more the fear began to melt from my body, and I started to tremble. A short distance off the path was a large rock I'd rested on many times, and I climbed to its flat, shaded top. I peeled off my makeshift bandage, wincing when the fabric stuck to the scraped skin. The swelling and redness were worse, and the urge to scratch my welts against the rock was unbearable.

The shuffle of leaves drew my acute ears and eyes. My muscles tensed, the hilt of the knife I always wore sheathed at my waist ready and snug in my palm.

There. In the mottled shadows, just beyond one of the larger trees, a figure darted away, their feet crunching in the bracken. Larger than my elven kin, muscular, with deep bronze skin and long, dark hair. The being disappeared into the underbrush.

I gasped at the renewed pounding pain between my temples, but I didn't take my eyes off the spot where the figure vanished. Each moment was an eternity as I sat, unmoving and silent.

It didn't reappear.

Was this my dark shadow?

It could have easily attacked. Maybe they were just biding their time, but, somehow, I didn't think so. To be sure, I waited until the waning sun teased the treetops. When the echo of my mother's stories of elves lost in the dark whispered in my ear, I resumed my walk, cradling my injured hand in my good one.

Lost in my thoughts, I bypassed the cottage completely and made my way down the steep cliffside stairs to a secluded beach I knew as well as I knew my own bedroom. The tide was coming in, and I knelt on the cove's dry sand, leaning forward on my hands so the waves lapped at them. The seawater instantly soothed the itchy brambleberry scratches, as my mother had advised me to do as a youngling.

I dug my fingers into the sand, grabbing handfuls that oozed out when I tightened my grip. The setting sun and sky reflected in the sea, turning the world brilliant reds and purples. The water was calm, but dark shapes breached the surface. Not fish, though too far out to identify. I saw them playing in the surf most every time I went to the beach.

I watched the silhouettes play until the rising tide reached my legs, soaking my breeches.

I was halfway up the stairs when a loud splash behind me caught my attention. When I turned, there was nothing.

No.

Wait.

Barely visible in the dimming light, smooth tracks swirled across the sand where my footprints had marred it just minutes before.

Heart in my throat, I raced up the stairs. I knew every shell, every grain of sand on this beach, yet never in my years had I seen a trail like that.

TWO

My mother's calm presence was a balm to my frayed nerves, though my mind still raced as I helped her finish the stew for our evening meal. A part of me worried she wouldn't be there when I arrived at the house after my detour to the beach.

"Kal, please stir so it doesn't stick." Mother twirled a finger in the air, and I smiled, imitating her with the spoon before attending to our dinner. "How were Lord Elmar's fields? It's been so hot," she said, pulling day-old bread from the cupboard.

"The same." I dislodged some stew from the bottom of the cast iron pot and added a little water.

Mother looked around furtively, then whispered, "Do you think it's a curse?"

I opened my mouth, then paused. Whereas yesterday I would have chuckled and told her she spent too much time losing herself in her books, today...

"I... I don't know." I sighed and told her about the mages Vulen and I had seen, swearing her to secrecy. "I hesitate to think the worst, but for now, I'm just glad whatever it is hasn't affected our crops." I gestured with the spoon to the robust haul Mother had harvested earlier.

She pursed her lips. "Mages. I don't like it. Not at all." She tore a chunk of bread for each of us as I dished the stew into bowls. "But I believe the gods have smiled upon our family before. They will again."

"Hmm. Perhaps." I didn't need something else to worry about. Along with the dark shadow, I'd been haunted by dreams—wisps, ghosts I couldn't capture—leaving me empty, alone and grasping. I awoke each morning convinced I'd lost something or that I'd been left behind. The dreams had plagued me over the years, more often of late.

Once we'd finished eating and washed, I retired to my room, eager to put the day behind me. Exhaustion overtook my senses, and it was only as I slid into relaxation that I realized I hadn't said a word to my mother about the strange figure in the forest.

I wrapped the bedding tightly around me and closed my eyes, letting the darkness pull me under.

WET SAND SQUISHED between my toes, cold and silky. The secluded cove at the base of the cliffs below my family's house seemed the same as ever, but when I looked down, my body was small, as though the passing years had melted away.

A splash behind me, followed by laughter, drew my curiosity. I turned toward the sound and a boy, bigger than me with tan skin and pointed ears like mine, crawled out of the surf. Another wave knocked him over, and he giggled. I rushed to help him up and found myself staring into the most vivid green eyes I'd ever seen.

"Hi," I said shyly. "I'm Kalysin." I looked around the beach—we were the only ones there. "Are you hurt? Where'd you come from?"

"Over there." The boy pointed out to sea. "I saw you playing and wanted to join you." He shook the clumps of sand from his feet. "I'm Laeroth, which is also my father's name, so don't call me that."

I nodded. "I'm called after mine too. He's away, trading with other lands." I dug my heel into the sand as my heart clenched. "Can I call you Roth? You can call me Kal if you want."

"Kal." Roth's lips tipped up in a smile. His canines were sharp and longer than mine, but not wildly so. "Want to look for shells?"

The afternoon seemed to pass in an instant, then Roth waved to me before swimming into the tide. Just where the deep water began, several figures bobbed, and I had the odd sensation I'd seen this before. As soon as Roth's small form reached them, they all dove, flashing fins, scales, tentacles, and tails. I stared, incredulous, until my eyes burned in the setting sun.

My mother found me on the beach, watching the waves and listening to the birds cry as dusk settled. "There you are, Kal. It's time to eat."

I grinned and looked up at her, her dark blond hair blowing in the wind. "I met a boy from the sea!" I pointed for good measure.

Her eyebrows rose as she tucked her hair behind a pointy ear, but she smiled indulgently. "From the sea? Well, be careful—your new playmate might not always play fair. Gods are fickle."

THE SAND SHIMMERED UNNATURALLY, and when I met Roth's eyes again, the cove and beach were scorchingly hot, and fat drops of cool water were falling from the sky. Years had passed in an instant. I was taller, my muscles starting to develop, and Roth was older, too—not a youngling, but not yet grown. His dark hair, longer than before, framed his face. Rivulets of rain ran down his neck. I turned my face to the dark clouds, unable to look at him for long. The rain washed the heat away, cooling my flushed skin.

"Is it always hot like this?" Roth asked me, lowering himself to sit on the smooth sand.

I mirrored his position. "During the summer, yes."

"It's so different from down there." He gestured over his shoulder toward the open water. "The temperature doesn't change much."

"Do you *really* live in the sea?" I raised an eyebrow. He'd explained, and I believed him, yet I enjoyed making him tell me. Something about the way his nose scrunched in frustration.

"*Yes*. Why? Do *you* really live up there?" Roth pointed up the stairs carved into the cliff face that led to my home.

"You *know* I do—you've been there, eaten from Mother's fruit bushes." I snorted—a rude, silly noise. "How do I know you're not just a trickster from some island down the coast, and the moment we see someone coming, you sneak off and run to your boat and disappear?" I playfully shoved his shoulder. "No one even believes me when I tell them about you. The other elves at the market say only gods could live in the water, and my mother says you're a figment of my very active imagination."

Roth poked me in the chest, his sharp white teeth flashing in the gray light. "Maybe *you're* the one who's not real."

I sat up straight, indignant. "Of course I am."

"Prove it."

My eyes darted to Roth's lips as he said the words, and before I could chicken out, I leaned forward, pressing my mouth to his. His face was covered in rain, but his skin was hot. I jerked back, and we stared at each other until Roth smiled.

"Very conclusive," he said seriously. "But maybe we should do it again to be sure."

As he leaned forward and put his hands on my shoulders, the world shimmered and tilted—

ROTH HAD me pinned to the sand on my back, the gentle tide bubbling around our ankles. His dark hair, longer than ever, had little braids woven throughout. My hands wandered of their own accord to his wide shoulders, though I had no urge to throw him off. When I squeezed my fingertips into his sun-warmed skin, the thick muscle beneath bunched and flexed with restrained power.

Just like his hips.

The youngling was no more. Roth was all man. And so was I.

Roth had been nude whenever he'd visited, while my state of dress had varied. But this time I was as naked as him.

He scored his sharp canines against the side of my neck in long lines, then soothed the scrape with his tongue. I trembled and whimpered and tilted my chin up, baring more of myself so he could do it again.

One of his hands slid roughly through the sand behind my long hair, and he cupped my nape. At the same time, he shrugged my hands off his shoulders and grasped both of my wrists so they were crossed together, stretching them above my head and holding them to the sand. The loss of control—or maybe because I'd allowed it to happen—fogged my senses.

"So beautiful like this," Roth whispered, his breath hot at my ear. "I've wanted to do this for so long, Kal."

I somehow knew I'd wanted the same.

"Yes," I hissed. "Please, Roth."

I planted one foot on the sand and canted my hips and Roth grunted as he drove down onto me, our cocks stiff and aching. I looped my other leg around his hip and rolled my pelvis, sweat and precum making the slide of our bodies effortless.

"Oh gods," I cried out, my back bowing against the earth as I struggled against his iron hold. But if I truly needed to be free, I knew Roth would let me go. With the hand on the back of my head, he guided my mouth to his as the pump of his cock against mine sent me over the edge. Warm wetness spread between us, and Roth gasped into my mouth as his cock marked my stomach as well.

"And now, little elf," Roth said, sinking his teeth into my lower lip, "you are mine."

"'Little elf'?" I turned my head and bit him on the shoulder to hide my smile. "I'll have you know I'm fully

—fully—grown." I swiveled my hips, drinking up the pleasure.

FLASH AFTER FLASH, encounters with Roth consumed my mind—I was on my knees in front of him, worshipping his cock with my mouth—

—sand ground into my palms as I clenched them into fists while he pumped into me from behind—

—my body nearly folded in half, legs thrown over his shoulders, Roth licking around my hole like it was a delicacy—

—treading water, his legs surrounding my face as he floated on his back, his cock pulsing as I jerked him off—

BETWEEN ONE INHALE and the next, the world spun again. The sun kissed the sea and our skin with late afternoon light.

Roth's hands squeezed mine. "Kal, I've pushed my luck too far, and I've been neglecting—" He shook his head, and I sensed I'd missed the beginning of the conversation. "This is the last time. I can't come to you anymore."

"Why?" My breath hitched, but I gained control of it again. "Can I go to you instead? I've never been—"

"It's not possible. We can't meet again. There are changes I'm about to go through, and my father…has need of me. And though you will not see me, I won't forget you. I'll never let anything hurt you." Roth cradled my cheek in a large hand, and I shamelessly pressed into it, trying to ignore the hole tearing open in my chest.

Confusion and anger swirled like a hurricane. "Am I to mourn you, then? No one will understand. Even after all these years, my mother tells me you don't exist. That you *can't*. That no one but the gods could—"

"I'm sorry." Roth's voice cracked.

His hollow expression broke me. This was somehow bigger than us.

"If that's how it has to be." My body shook, but not from any cold. "I'll remember you always," I choked out.

"No, little elf." Roth's eyes glazed with unshed tears. "You won't."

He kissed me on the forehead, and, as he strode into the waves, my knees gave out and the world went dark.

I AWOKE, drenched in sweat and twisted in my bedding, yet still feeling the sand beneath my feet. Those dreams —I'd been having them for months. But this was the first time they'd still been imprinted in my mind upon waking, solid and clear as though they'd just happened.

There was no way they were dreams. They had to be memories.

Wetness trickled down my face, and I swiped away the tears. Predawn light shone through the open window, more than enough to see cooled seed on my stomach—

And the smooth, tan skin on my hand where bramble-berry scratches had been just hours before.

THREE

Too anxious to fall back to sleep, I cleaned up and dressed. I had to get out of there, move, do something, anything. Going down to the beach was out of the question—my mind had spent hours there with the love of my life who had left me.

In a haze, I started the slow walk to Lord Elmar's estate. These were memories—*my* memories. Why had they been taken from me? Why had they returned?

I was consumed with thoughts of Roth, pushing everything else to the periphery. How had someone who had meant so much to me been...erased? Like he'd never existed? He'd been the one raiding my mother's berry bushes with me. Who'd collected the shells filling a deep bowl in my bedroom. Who'd claimed me as his on the shores of the cove, the border between our lands.

My skin went hot remembering his touch, his mouth, his hardness. The way I lit up for him when he pinned me to the sand, using his bulk to keep me where he wanted me.

And then... Had *he* been the one to steal my memories? My chest clenched tight. I glanced at my newly healed hand. What was Roth hiding? What hadn't he told me?

I stopped mid-step, right in the middle of the road, and a rider swore at me as he directed his horse around. I moved to the side, sipping from my waterskin until my lungs loosened. What did it matter, anyway? Roth only existed in my memories. For a moment, I wished the memories had stayed locked away.

I resumed my trek with lead feet.

A cart thundered down the trail. It pulled even with me, then blocked me from walking farther. I stumbled back a few steps, my hand going for my knife before I saw who it was. My hand relaxed at my side.

"Kalysin. I'm glad you're early," Horith, one of Elmar's chief advisors, said from the driver's seat. "His lordship requested I fetch you. He's expecting a full report on your findings."

My stomach sank to my toes. None of the news I had for Lord Elmar would please him. Best to accept it. And if he released me from his service, it wouldn't be the worst thing.

Horith whisked me away to the manor. The grand home was in the middle of a curated forest planted ages ago. It was open to the elements for the most part, towering trees providing cover where concealed roofs did not.

"He's in the conservatory." Horith stopped the cart near the massive marble steps leading to the manor's main entrance. I let myself in through a side door used by the staff and made my way to the room Lord Elmar prized above all else—where he spent his days reading, studying, and tending his favorite plants.

The conservatory was roofed by the massive trees outside, the leafy canopy so thick sunlight barely reached through. What illumination there was in the room was provided by a glowing orb floating high above the room's center. Sweat beaded at my hairline—for the plants, the room was far warmer and humid than it was outside at this time of day. My gut was already churning, and the heat didn't help.

Lord Elmar's tall, wiry figure was clad in an ornate robe and hunched over a spine-covered plant from which he was plucking palm-sized purple fruit with long, dexterous fingers.

"Ah, Kalysin." Lord Elmar handed the fruit to a servant, to whom he said, "Have these prepared for our celebratory feast this evening." The servant nodded, bowed, and removed a basket overflowing with fruit from the room, leaving the two of us alone.

"My lord." I gave a short bow and decided to make my report. For all his love of pageantry, Lord Elmar did appreciate efficiency. "I've walked every path on your lands and—"

"Yes, yes, I know. There's a drought. The crops are sickly. Failing. Nothing you've done has worked, and you've not discovered the cause." He rubbed a pointed ear. "Nature is difficult to control. My concern is that this may not be...natural."

I frowned. "What do you mean, my lord?"

"That this is something the gods have wrought upon us. Perhaps we have displeased them in some way."

"You believe the gods are...punishing us?"

"Precisely." Lord Elmar pursed his thin lips. "Once upon a time, rumor was you had their ear. Could speak to the gods. Could influence their actions if you were given the right...incentive."

Did he truly believe those ridiculous stories from when I was young? Roth was no god. I reflexively stroked my knife's wooden hilt with my thumb. This conversation was becoming increasingly unhinged. Just yesterday I was practically to blame for the drought, and now it was the gods' fault?

Guards filtered into the conservatory, pairing up at the doors. One eye on the soldiers, I chose my words carefully.

"Respectfully, my lord—for years, I was lonely, with just my mother for companionship. Any friends were my mind's own creation—I was never truly able to speak to the gods. I regret the rumors were distorted to suggest this."

Lord Elmar's mouth twisted into a mockery of a smile. "And yet, I am willing to take the chance." He gestured, and the guards surrounded me. All were armed, though they had not drawn their weapons.

"What's the meaning of this?" I tensed, searching for an escape, but they were in a tight formation.

"You, Kalysin, are going to be sacrificed to ensure a bountiful harvest."

The mages I'd seen in the field appeared and silently flanked Lord Elmar.

My mouth dropped open, but no sound came out.

"I've followed the rumors since you were a youngling. And it was so convenient of you to come to me for work —much simpler to keep you close for when a day like this arrived."

The mages waved their hands in unison and my body locked up, held motionless with magic. Two of the guards grabbed my shoulders and I struggled within my invisible prison. Several others drew their swords, pushing in close. One took my knife.

"I refuse," I growled through clenched teeth. While I didn't follow my peoples' religion like my mother did, I knew enough—only a willing sacrifice would achieve the desired results.

"Then your mother will be your replacement." Lord Elmar approached with a Seeing Stone. Inside the sphere I saw my mother in our fields. A moment later, several of Lord Elmar's guards grabbed her. She wrenched from their grip, falling and tipping over a full basket, the day's harvest spilling in the dirt.

My blood ran cold. I'd been so wrapped up in my dreams and memories of Roth I'd left that morning without even speaking to her.

Lord Elmar sneered. "Clearly the gods *are* smiling on you if your meager lands can produce like this while mine *wither*, despite my best attempts."

"Don't hurt her." My pulse pounded in my ears. "I'll willingly die on your altar, but you have to release her first. Unharmed." She would be safe. I had to believe that.

Lord Elmar tilted his head and leaned in toward me. "Done."

Roth had made his choice years ago, and it broke my heart. Good thing he wasn't around to hear me make mine.

CHAPTER

FOUR

As soon as I accepted, Lord Elmar had me taken to an empty room that was better-appointed than the house my mother and I shared.

My stomach curdled, and I sat heavily in one of the ridiculously upholstered chairs, wrinkling the long white linen tunic and pants I'd been given. The sacrifice to the gods couldn't happen in my usual light breeches and shirt—for this to work, they needed to do this by the book.

There was a disturbance outside in the hallway, then the door opened just enough for a figure to wedge into the gap. Dark blond hair tangled and her face dirty, my mother was spitting fire.

"Unhand me, you barbaric—Kal?" Her eyes widened as she saw me dressed in the sacrificial garb. She made to enter the room but was held back by someone with a leather-clad arm. "Are you all right? They haven't hurt you? These brutes took me this morning." She glared over her shoulder.

I shook my head, tears filling my eyes. "I'm not hurt, Mother." I walked up to the door and looked her over as best I could, taking her hand. "Are you?"

"I'll live." She squeezed my fingers. "Kal, what have you agreed to?"

"Don't—don't worry about me." My voice trembled, and I gripped her hand like it was my lifeline. "Everything's going to be fine."

Her eyebrows rose. "Kal, what did—"

"Enough," a rough voice growled. Someone dragged my mother back, and her hand was ripped from my clutches. "You've seen she's alive and unharmed."

"Kal!"

"Mother!"

The door slammed in my face.

Interminable minutes later, one of the guards stuck his head in. "It's time."

I sighed deeply and didn't move.

"Don't make this worse for yourself," the guard said, his voice hard.

"Or what?" I got up and plodded toward the door barefoot. I hadn't been given shoes, and my clothing had been taken from me when I changed. "You'll kill me?"

"No, I'll have to kill *her*." The guard's face softened for a brief moment as he glanced around the room. "I've got a youngling who will starve if the crops fail." He met my eyes and seemed to steel himself. Manacles dangled from his fingers. "Come along now."

Once I was cuffed, an armored escort led me to a part of Lord Elmar's vast property I'd never seen. Hidden within concentric circles of trees was a group of small temples, one for each of the gods. Sweet-smelling flowers and vines grew around them, well-tended by acolytes. This area hadn't been in my realm of responsibilities. An odd, detached part of me wondered who would make sure the harvest went smoothly once I was gone, but it probably wouldn't matter if my sacrifice was successful.

In the center, between the temples and trees, was a large altar, the gray stone slab carved, ancient, and polished. My vision narrowed in on the flat top—would its shiny surface be the last thing I'd ever see? I wavered on my feet and closed my eyes, convinced I could hear the sea crashing on the shore. But when I opened them again, the soothing sound of the tide continued. Not my imagination, then—we must be close to the water.

My legs stopped moving as I approached the altar, and a guard shoved me forward with the butt of his spear. All at once, the guards lifted me, slamming me down on my back on top of the altar, knocking the air from my lungs. I struggled to recover my breath as they chained me to the stone, taking no chances I'd run.

Lord Elmar appeared at my side, an intricately carved dagger in his hand and a cruel smirk on his face. The mages surrounded the altar, joining hands and softly chanting. "Kalysin, you'll be giving me more than you know. Understand that I, and the gods, appreciate your sacrifice."

He raised the dagger, and I wrestled against the chains, but there was no slack or give.

I was going to die.

I closed my eyes and listened to the sea.

Used my last moments to remember the way Roth had held me.

Told me I was his.

FIVE

Hot coppery wetness splashed my face, and I waited to feel pain that never came.

The ring of steel filled my ears, the clang of wood and metal mixing with yells of rage and cries of pain. Blood overpowered the temples' flowers, turning the scent sickly sweet. I retched and cracked open my eyes to the sight of spears flying and Lord Elmar's guards falling like toy soldiers to— Was I hallucinating? Tall, strong people wearing light, leathery armor were annihilating my captors with spears, daggers, and short swords.

A shadow covered my face, and I flinched away, the chains clinking.

"Easy there." A familiar deep voice met my ears, and I stared up into the beautiful emerald eyes I'd seen the night before in my dreams. Was this real? It had to be.

His body was covered in dark tattoos I'd never seen on him before.

"Roth," I breathed. "You're here."

Though years had passed, it was like time hadn't touched his gorgeous face. Roth grinned. "Yes, little elf. I always intended to come back to you. But I didn't know when I could."

Roth and some of his companions broke the chains holding me. I sat up and swung my legs over the side of the slab, rubbing my wrists.

"How? You left, and then, at the exact moment I was to be—" I choked on the word *sacrificed*. "You came to my aid."

"I promised no one would hurt you. I will tell you everything, Kalysin. I promise that too."

Roth brought my chafed wrists to his lips. The skin tingled, healing in an instant. We were eye-level, and, before I could second guess myself, I pulled him to me, his big body crowding between my spread legs. I slid a hand to the nape of his neck and dragged him in, claiming him with my mouth. He tasted the same. It occurred to me this was the first time I'd seen him wear... anything. I couldn't hold back a laugh. "You're real."

He kissed me back. "So are you."

I swiped at my face. "Whose blood is..." I trailed off as I looked down to see Lord Elmar lying on the ground, disarmed, held at spearpoint by one of my saviors, and pressing his hand to a nasty wound at his neck. The mages were nowhere to be seen now that this monster had been captured.

"Hold him," Roth ordered the soldiers, "on the grounds of tampering with nature's balances through arcane means. And, more importantly, attempting to murder the mate of King Laeroth the Third. May justice be done."

My jaw dropped. "Mate? Me? What?"

"Your highness," said one of Roth's soldiers. "You must take him to the shore."

Without another word, Roth picked me up, and though I was not small for a woodland elf, I felt secure in his arms. He ran with me to the secluded cove where we'd met many years before and deposited me on the sand like I was something precious. He lay down next to me, and my heart squeezed—it was just like my dreams.

Roth took the hand that had been scratched by the brambleberry bush. He idly stroked the smooth, unmarred skin.

"Did you heal me last night?"

"Yes, Kal. I couldn't stay away." He sighed. "A lot has happened since we last parted. I've always been my people's prince, but when I was with you, I could just be *me*. And my father—I was telling you the truth long ago when I said he had need of me. He was dying, Kal, and he needed me to learn to rule, to take my place among my people." Roth drew lazy patterns on the sand. "And to choose a mate. But I'd already chosen *you*." He leaned in and our lips met, slow and sensual.

"Then why did you leave? And take my memories?" Bitterness stained my voice.

He clenched his jaw. "All my father's doing. You were the first ever land-based mate for any of our people. My father ordered it done, forbade me from seeing you, hoping it would break our bond and I'd mate with one of our own. He wanted me to take the crown and the throne with a proper mate." Roth stroked my hair, and I leaned into his touch.

"And you...didn't?"

"No. You were all I ever wanted. After my father died and I still refused anyone but you, my advisors were peculiarly desperate to figure out a way to reunite us properly. And once our mages sensed a growing threat from your lands, I needed to ensure your safety." Roth mouthed at my neck.

"Because of the increasing danger from Lord Elmar, I was compelled to make contact with you, see you, heal you. I believe the memory spell didn't last because we're mates. I'm sorry, little elf, my mate, for all the pain."

I filled my lungs with the sea air, still marveling that I was alive. "I've never felt as whole as when I woke this morning, my memories of you restored. I can't live without you again."

Roth pursed his lips and glanced down at the sand. "There was…something else. Another reason I had to leave to be with my people."

"And that was…?"

He sat up and took a deep breath. I mirrored his position and basked in the early afternoon sun warming my body. I'd long since stopped shaking in fear, but the chill in my bones had remained.

"My people…we're not like you."

I cocked my head. "I'm not following."

Roth smiled. "We go through a second transformation after we're fully physically mature. Our city is beneath the waves, and our transformation reflects that. After, we can shift at will between forms, but must return to the water after a time. Land cannot be my permanent home."

"So you turn into…a fish?"

Roth's face when he broke into laughter was incandescent. "Some do, little elf, but only their bottom half." He put a large hand on my belly, stroking the white linen shirt. "We take on different forms, depending on our family lines. You may remember seeing some of us play in the water?"

I nodded, recalling silhouettes of fins and tails and the flash of scales on the waves.

"My family—"

"—the *royal* family?" I interrupted, still incredulous.

"Yes, the royal family, is no different. Would you like to see?" His hands twisted over the leather armor of his lap, and I knew Roth well enough to realize he was nervous yet trying not to show it.

"Laeroth." I looked him straight in the eye. "If I've learned anything, it's that I will love you whether I remember you or not, and in whatever form you take. *Show me.*"

SIX

Roth backed away from me on his knees, carefully removed his protective clothing, and retreated into the waves. His big body glistened, the dark tattoos following his muscles. I drank in the sight of him, still wondering if this was an exceptionally vivid dream. I didn't want to wake up if it was.

He beckoned, and I followed until I was up to my knees in the water. Roth held a hand up, halting me when he was a little over waist deep. There was a bright flash, and the water surged, roiling and churning around him. I moved forward again, fascinated. I only looked down when something brushed my ankle. A deep purple tentacle moved in the water as though afraid to touch me again.

"*Oh*," I said, staring, and knelt in the shallows, soaking the thin white linen pants. I could practically feel Roth's eyes on me as I reached in and gently grazed the tentacle with my fingertips. When it didn't retreat, I picked it up as I stood.

The appendage was pure muscle and tapered down to a delicate tip that curled around my fingers with ease. Now out of the water, the color varied from violet to indigo, and even an intense gray. Suction cups ran along one side, gripping my arm. The surface wasn't slimy as I would have expected, but soft, velvety.

"Beautiful," I whispered, and the tentacle shivered.

"I'm glad you think so," Roth said, voice full of relief as he waded closer to me, "because there are more of them. I'm one of the cecaeliae. Octo-folk, we're sometimes called."

The tentacle gently guided me farther into the shallows until Roth could take my hand in one of his. His body appeared to change around his hips, the deep V of his pelvis and bronze of his skin gradually merging with the violet of his second shape. I pressed my other hand to his abdomen, repeating what he had done to me just minutes before, delighted when the muscles quivered.

"How many do you have?" I asked, gazing up at him.

"Eight. And then there's…" Roth paused. "I'm not— shaped—the same as when I'm in my two-legged form." Was he blushing? "But I can do everything in this form I can do in my other."

"What—*oh*." My eyes widened. "And how do you know?" I wasn't sure I wanted to hear the answer.

"Because, little elf, my family told me. That was quite a conversation. But rest assured, there's been no one else but you, in either of my forms. It's always been only you."

"So, you've never..." I licked my lips, my face flushed. "Would you like to?"

"Yes," Roth breathed. "Let's create new memories."

The tentacle unwound from my arm and slid around my back, urging me forward into Roth's space. He sank a little so we were face-to-face, his green eyes scanning me like he wanted to memorize my features. How I'd gone so long without seeing him, remembering him... Never again. We loved each other and would find a way—woodland elves were resourceful, and my mate was octo-folk royalty.

His scent was the same, of warm musky skin and salty seawater, and I was instantly transported back to the countless other times I was this close to him. Laeroth. My mate.

I threaded my fingers into his long hair, taking care not to pull any of the little braids woven throughout, and took his mouth with a moan. Heat flashed down my spine. No wonder my memories had returned—I would know the taste of him, the feel of him, the very presence of him, anywhere.

"Promise me," I whispered, dragging my lips over his cheek. "Promise you'll always come back to me."

"I promise, Kal. But I plan to never leave you again."

Our open mouths crashed together, his tongue dominating. I sucked him in but threw my head back with a gasp when Roth's hands roamed from my neck down to my chest where the wet linen stuck to my body like a second skin. Deft fingers plucked at my nipples through the fabric, both too rough and not enough. After so long without his hands on me, it was like the little nubs were connected straight to my cock. I arched into his touch and nearly lost my balance, but his tentacles supported me, keeping me upright in the gentle waves.

With a growl, Roth grabbed my shirt at the neckline with both hands and ripped the linen straight down the middle. His tentacles nimbly helped me out of it, throwing the ruined fabric into the sea. Maybe it would be lost, fading as my memories of this terrible day were as Roth consumed me.

"You were always quite fond of this..." Roth grinned, exposing those long canines. He dipped his head, scoring my water-cooled skin, then lapping up each line with his warm tongue.

I squirmed against him, desperate for friction. "Please."

Gentle pressure at each wrist guided my arms up, and, without thinking, I bent my elbows over my head and pressed my wrists together. Smooth purple flesh wrapped them, freezing me in place and urging me to relax back into Roth's supporting tentacles.

"Oh," I moaned, my mind fuzzy with the release of letting go. Of giving Roth complete control. Even though I wasn't sure where this was taking us, I was along for the ride.

"Yes, Kal. I know." Roth hummed next to my ear. "You're gorgeous like this, tanned from the sun, body firm from your hard work." My eyes went wide at his words. He bared his teeth. "Oh yes, I've been watching you. Now, let me give you what you need." He bit my neck where it met my shoulder, and I cried out, my stance widening, wordlessly begging for him to touch me.

He dragged a hand down my chest to the laces on the linen pants, but didn't untie them. My cock strained against the translucent material. He chuckled and rubbed his thumb over my erection, tracing the veins and the sensitive crown. So close already. Too close. I hadn't been touched by anyone except my own hands since Roth and was going to come apart quickly, like I had our first time. I rocked my hips, kept at his mercy by the strong appendages gripping my arms. His chuckle became a full-on laugh, and I bit my lip to keep from begging.

Feather-light fingertips grazed my cock, the sensation through the fabric like nothing I'd felt before, like the barrier was my skin. Roth stroked tiny circles right under the head, barely moving his hand. I shook from head to toe as I rode the wave of euphoria higher.

He stared, watching his hand on me like this was the most important thing he would ever do. "Give in, Kal.

This won't be our last time. Not even today. I have *plans* for us."

Oh yes. I needed everything, all of him. I cried out as blissful agony tore me apart. Roth's tentacles held me firmly in place as my cock kicked and pulsed, streaming cum into the linen while he barely touched me. I melted, unable to even feel embarrassed.

Roth lowered his head and licked the stained linen. "You're perfect."

I needed the pants gone immediately. His touch on my body with nothing in between us. But Roth took his time loosening the ties.

He loomed over my heaving chest. "I'm in no hurry, Kal. I've been dreaming of this day. Let me take you slow."

"Oh gods."

Roth lowered the pants over my hips, and the tentacles took over, shifting the wet fabric until it was off my feet. It joined the shirt somewhere in the waves.

Velvet crept up my legs, wrapping around my thighs until I was spread open to him. Curious, I tried to bring my thighs together, but the incredible strength of the tentacles kept me positioned as he wanted me. I hovered, seated and leaning back, completely at his mercy.

One of the purple tentacles around my legs extended its tip toward my cock, teasing as Roth had with his thumb. Up and down, then around and around it circled, making a tight ring around the base of my cock and balls. My erection throbbed with my heartbeat.

Something firm and tactile teased my hole, and I instinctively clenched.

"Relax your body, Kal. I need to make you ready for me."

Roth gripped me by the waist with both hands, his thumbs stroking my stomach. The tentacle touched me, skirting around the rim, reminding me of how Roth had spent a whole afternoon tasting me there, opening me up until he could slip his fingers in. The width was similar to one of his fingers, and soon I took it easily. I bit my lip when the appendage undulated and curled, gently massaging me from the inside.

"Yes," I hissed when it brushed against a spot that made me shiver.

"I love what happens when I tease you there." Roth nipped at my neck. "Breathe, Kal."

He moved one of his hands to where we were connected, kneading, relaxing, loosening. A moment later, his tentacle retreated, leaving me surprisingly empty. I tried to sit up, ready to beg, but a surge of pressure had me arching my back as something thicker stretched the tight ring of muscle.

"That's it," Roth murmured. "Take all of me."

There was no resistance as what I assumed was his cock conquered my body as though it belonged there. Roth groaned, drawing his hips back and thrusting forward, working his thickness inside. I'd never been so full. Roth petted my lower abs and shifted his hips. My eyes widened as a slight bulge on my stomach moved when his cock withdrew.

Oh gods.

My mouth dropped open in a feral cry, nearly delirious by this claiming. I needed him. I needed *this*.

"Roth, please," I begged, lungs sucking in air. "Own me, mark me, make me yours."

"And I will."

We made our own waves as he pounded into me, taking as much as I gave. The purple bands around my arms and thighs were the only things stopping me from flinging myself around his body and riding him as we floated there.

The angle of his thrusts changed slightly, the bulbous head sliding against that incredible spot. All at once, his grip tightened everywhere, holding me still as his cock swelled. Roth flung his head back and roared, warmth flooding my passage.

My own cock strained, the tentacle still curled around the base and my balls. Before I could say anything, he withdrew from me and pushed a tentacle inside my hole again. The girth was almost too much as he pressed the sensitive spot inside, relentless. All my limbs quivered as he pleasured me, eyes locked on mine until he released the tentacle ringing my cock. Blood flow resumed, and I screamed in euphoria, my untouched cock spurting onto my chest and his abdomen like a fountain.

"Beautiful," Roth said, dragging his fingers through my release before licking them. His grip on me relaxed, just enough for me to embrace the boneless, weightless feeling, both in my head and in the water around me. With minute adjustments, Roth slid me into his arms. I anchored myself with my legs around his waist and arms hugging his shoulders, then kissed him slowly.

Another flash of light, and I felt his feet hit the sand, but all I knew was the comfort of his skin pressed against mine. He walked us to the beach and lowered us to the sand, arranging me so I faced away from him, then moved in close behind, holding my back to his chest.

I gasped when he lifted my top leg and slipped his cock into my stretched hole, my body swallowing him entirely as we loved each other into the afternoon.

Hours later, I laid with my head on Roth's broad chest, admiring his swirling tattoos and watching the sunset.

"So, what is your plan now?" I asked, idly tracing patterns around his peaked nipples while he carded his fingers through my long, dark hair. Roth had said earlier he wouldn't leave me again, but I couldn't see how that was possible. He was a king now, and I couldn't survive in his kingdom.

"We're mates, Kal. And everyone knows a ruler is most effective when they have their loved ones by their side." Roth smiled gently and gestured to the sea with his chin. "Look."

Out on the water, the dark outline of a figure expertly navigated the waves. When they reached the shallows, they nodded to us. Roth rose first, then helped me up. We walked, hand in hand, into the water. The figure's lower half was hard to see, but a long, fish-like tail swayed with the tide.

"Kal, this is Marious, my most trusted mage. They've created a spell—one that will allow you to breathe under water and help your body adjust to the sea."

My eyes widened. "So I can join you?"

"Yes, little elf. We belong to each other now."

"Will I be able to visit my mother?"

"Of course. I would never keep you from her."

Under the stars, the spell was cast, and Roth dragged his teeth against my neck. The skin tingled, but not in the usual way—I gasped as gills formed where his mouth had been.

He crushed me to his big body and pressed his lips to mine, then I followed my love into the waves.

My mother was right—the gods had smiled upon me after all.

EPILOGUE

ONE YEAR LATER

I surfaced on the beach, Laeroth close behind but struggling to keep up with my excited steps.

"Eager?" He laughed as I led him up the stairs on the cliff face.

"Of course I am. It's been a month since I've seen her." I glanced around my mother's property as we followed the path to the house. The small fields were ripe with the fruits of her labors.

Last summer, after Lord Elmar had tried to eliminate me, my Roth, King Laeroth the Third—though I rarely thought of him that way—had coordinated with other elvish lords to discover what happened.

With a hefty dose of truth serum, Elmar confessed it all. He'd somehow found out about Roth's and my companionship as younglings and assumed I could talk to the gods. And he wanted that power for himself.”

Convinced the place I communed with the gods was sacred, Elmar was intent on possessing it. He'd concocted an insane plan to cause a drought that would affect only my poor family's land hoping, if things became dire enough, my mother or I would sell it to him.

Or we'd just leave and he'd swoop in and take it.

What Elmar hadn't counted on was Roth convincing his mages to place a protective spell on our home in one of his first acts as king. When Elmar's mages attacked, their spell backfired and cursed his own vast lands with the drought he'd so badly wanted.

Sacrificing me was his last desperate effort to either appease the gods or eliminate one of the owners of the lands he desired. He'd admitted if I'd died that day, he would have broken his word to me and had my mother disposed of immediately, never to be found.

Elmar was stripped of his title and imprisoned far away, his lands divided up among his workers and the neighboring properties.

“Mother?” I called out as I opened the door to the cottage. The windows were open, letting in the fresh sea breeze.

“Kal, Roth!” she said. “We're out here by the fire.”

“*We?*” I whispered to Roth. “Who's *we?*”

He adjusted his breeches—I'd managed to convince him to wear them each time we'd visited, telling him this form was so gorgeous he might well make my mother's heart stop if he arrived naked—and kissed me on the forehead. "Perhaps she's found someone to make her days a little brighter, little elf."

"Maybe." My lips twitched. It was high time the gods smiled on my mother too.

Acknowledgments

As always, thank you to my husband for being my best cheerleader. I love you!

Thank you to the Red Reines for making the tastiest sausage.

Thank you to Leslie Morris Noyes for the amazing cover.

Thank you to Red Quill Editing for whipping this story into shape.

Thank you to Passionate Ink for coordinating an amazing charity anthology, for which this story was originally written.

And thank you to my readers who make it all worthwhile.

About the Author

Ryley Banks writes award-winning bestselling spicy romance, mostly of the LGBTQ+ variety. She's a connoisseur of tea and gin and loves language, especially creative profanity.

When she's not begging her characters to behave or reading fanfic, you can find Ryley watching cooking how-to videos, traveling, or, if you're lucky, crafting the next story to make you smile and set you on fire.

Stay up to date on all of Ryley's releases by subscribing to her VIP reader newsletter. https://ryleybanks.com/ryleys-vip-newsletter/ Subscribers receive a free novelette, *Heat Waves*.

Visit Ryley at: https://ryleybanks.com/

facebook.com/RyleyBAuthor

instagram.com/ryleybauthor

bookbub.com/authors/ryleybanks

goodreads.com/ryleybanks

Also by Ryley Banks

Find all of Ryley's books:

Or go to: https://ryleybanks.com/books/

Anthologies

Hot & Sticky: A Passionate Ink Anthology (featuring *Heat Waves*)

Holiday Shorts: A Passionate Ink Anthology (featuring *O is for Ornament*)

Falling Hard: A Passionate Ink Anthology (featuring *Hard Cider Crush*)

The Big Book of Orgasms Volume 2: 69 Sexy Stories (featuring *Third Time's the Charm*)

Ink: Queer Sci Fi's Eighth Annual Flash Fiction Contest (featuring *Right Place, Right Time*)

Nonfiction

Demystifying the Beats: How to Write a Killer Book by Carol Potenza, Jordyn Kross, Ryley Banks, and Erin Krueger

RYLEY'S VIP READER LIST

Sign up for Ryley's VIP reader list and get her latest new release news, updates, deals, freebies, and giveaways!

Or go to: https://www.ryleybanks.com/ryleys-vip-newsletter

www.ingramcontent.com/pod-product-compliance
Lightning Source LLC
Chambersburg PA
CBHW061553310726
48972CB00008B/2734